GOODNIGHT OPUS

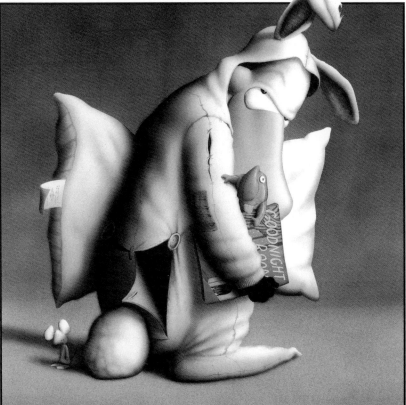

BERKELEY BREATHED

People who never get carried away should be. — Malcolm Forbes

Little, Brown and Company

Boston Toronto London

For Caity Mac and Maggie May — text-departing experts

Also by Berkeley Breathed

The Last Basselope

A Wish for Wings That Work: An Opus Christmas Story

First Edition

ISBN 0-316-10853-7
Library of Congress Catalog Card Number 93-7869

10 9 8 7 6 5 4 3 2 1

LAKE

Published simultaneously in Canada
by Little, Brown & Company (Canada) Limited

Printed in the United States of America

This work of fine literature is not suggested for use by an adult unless accompanied by a kid or a kid guardian. If a suitable minor cannot be located, a proper set of bunny jammies should be worn during the reading. Please help us maintain these minimal standards.

"Which book, dear Opus, may I read you tonight?"
asked Grandma with love at the start of that night.
"Why, my favorite," I said, "the one with the rhymes,
the same one you've read me two hundred nine times."

And just as it is with all proper grannies,
she ordered me into my pink bunny jammies.
Then she sat and said, "Hush," and her voice filled the room.
"Goodnight," she read softly,
"goodnight to the moon…

"And goodnight to the lamp and the little toy boat,
goodnight to the mittens all hanging and soaked.
Goodnight to the floor, goodnight to the walls,
goodnight to the rug and the door and the halls.
Goodnight tiny mouse and goodnight blue moonshine,
goodnight!" Grandma read, the two hundred tenth time.

I can't really say how this happened next:
After two hundred ten times,
I departed the text…

"Goodnight," I yelled, jumping, "goodnight far away.
Goodnight to you all in my Milky Way!"

"Sit back down," Grandma said, "get back into bed.
There's *no one* up there and that's *not* what I read.
When your sight surpasses what's plainly in view,
pull your head from the clouds, keep the ground to your shoes.

"Now let's finish the story with no Milky Way.
It's improper that folks get so carried away."

But she read no further,
she said nothing more.
Yes, Grandma had paused
for a snooze and a snore.

Now, I take full blame
for all that came next.
For I continued the story…

...but departed the text.

Goodnight!" I yelled down to the chap 'neath my bed.
"Goodnight to you, big-nosed blue-footed biped!
I'm so sorry I've missed you each night but tonight.
I was told not to focus on things out of sight."

"Yes, goodnight," said the beast with the toes taffy blue.
"I've been here for years and not noticed *you*!

"Let's finish your story and get carried away.
We'll wish them goodnight in that far Milky Way."
My friend winked to me as his voice dropped to whispers:
"Let's go there *ourselves,* wish it right to their kissers!"

"A team's what we need!" That's just what I said,
so we signed up my pillow and gave him a head.

But what of dear Grandma? There's no need to tell her.
We hoisted and snuck her down to the fruit cellar.
She'd hear nothing there as she snored in her slumber,
comfy and snug under tons of cucumber.

Our crew was complete, my Milky Way team.
We boarded our Milky Way flying machine.
Powered by dreams, with some blue-footed help,
we launched from the roof and let out a yelp:
"Goodnight to the city! Goodnight all you people!"
Then we sideswiped a kitty and shortened a steeple.

We flew past a fairy in need of some sleep —
she'd spent the whole night just collecting old teeth.
They rose to her girdle and covered her feet;
there were heaps upon heaps, two thousand feet deep.
"Goodnight!" we yelled down and she waved us over.
She wished to resell an old Elvis molar.

We dropped in to check on the Washington scene,
where I talked with Abe Lincoln and told him our scheme.
He said he himself had chased a few dreams,
but now that he's marble, he wished for small things.
"And what," I then asked, "would you most like to do?"
"A swan dive," he said, so we stripped and did two.

We flew past the sailors of Blue Mist Lagoon,
where for ten thousand years they've fished for the moon.
They've seen it up there and they just want to hook it.
They dream that one day they might baste it and cook it.
"Goodnight!" I called down. "We'd help but we're late.
We're off to the stars." And they yelled, "Bring some bait!"

We flew through the clouds, and that's where we met
all those wonderful folks aboard that big jet.
We yelled them goodnight 'til our faces turned purple,
but theirs turned to *white*, like they'd swallowed a gerbil.
We haven't a clue as to what caused the scare —
they slipped by quite nicely with inches to spare.

Then we soared higher up 'til the whole sky was filled
with lovable friends that the Milky Way spilled.

There, all above us, six billion udders.
No cow dads around, just milky cow mudders.
"Goodnight!" I cried out. "Goodnight one and all!"
Then they served us ice cream for a Milky Way ball.

T'was time to go home and they wept and said no,
then they kissed us goodnight, all six billion or so.
So here is the freshest of up-to-now tips:
If you're due a cow smooch, avoid those cow lips.

I found my way home and collapsed on the floor,
not long before Grandma showed up at the door.
I told her all of what happened that night —
that I stepped out for once and followed my sight.
And that sometimes it's good that we look for a way
to depart from our text and get carried away.

For years I've thought back to how Grandma had listened
to all the great things that I said she'd been missin'.
How that night she had paused at the foot of my bed,
and *smiled* at those Milky Way cows overhead.
I sure like to think that one night or the next…

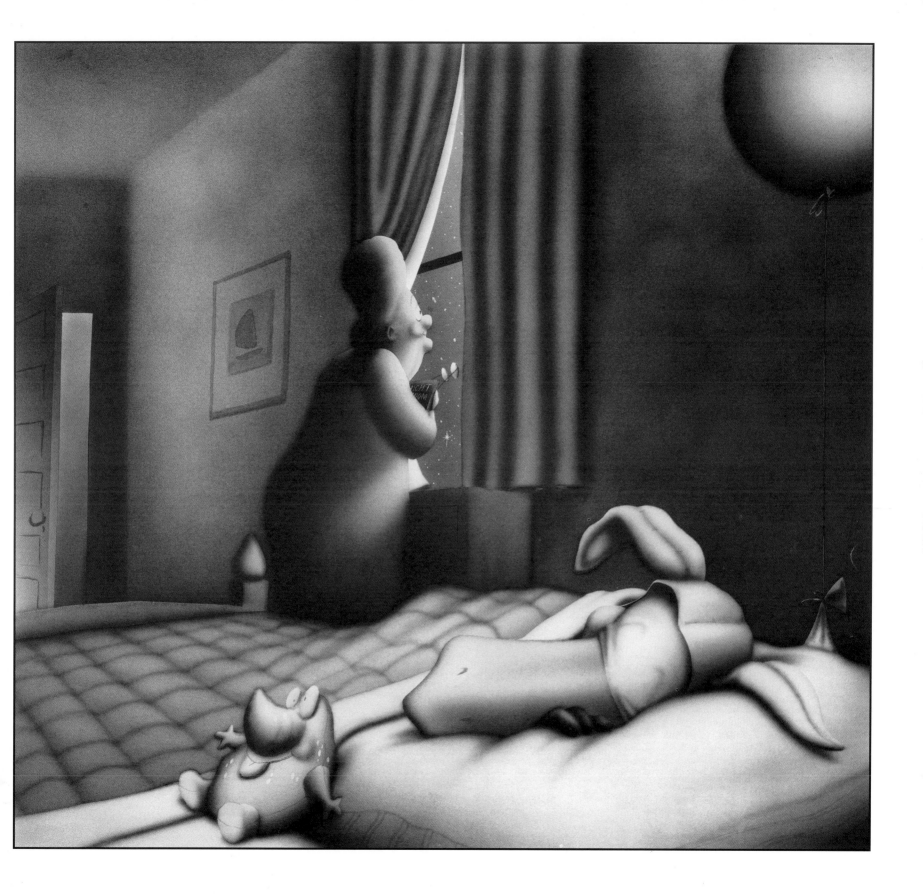

...she'll get carried away
and depart from the text.